Jack Nesbit

The Volcano Files: Poison Island & Volcanic Panic
published in 2008 by
Hardie Grant Egmont
85 High Street
Prahran, Victoria 3181, Australia
www.hardiegrantegmont.com.au

*The pages of this book are printed on paper approved by the
Forest Stewardship Council (FSC), which promotes responsible management
of the world's forests.*

A CiP record for this title is available from the National Library of Australia

Poison Island first published in 2006
Volcanic Panic first published in 2008

Cover illustration and design by Andy Hook

Printed in China

1 3 5 7 9 10 8 6 4 2

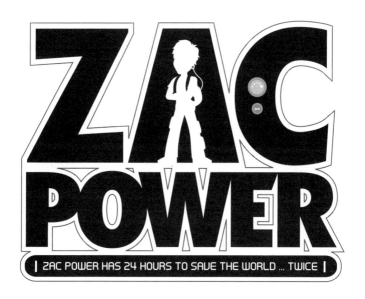

ZAC POWER HAS 24 HOURS TO SAVE THE WORLD ... TWICE

THE VOLCANO FILES

POISON ISLAND
& VOLCANIC PANIC

BY *H. I. LARRY*

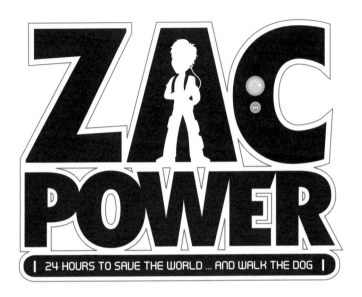

POISON ISLAND

BY *H. I. LARRY*

ILLUSTRATIONS BY *ASH OSWALD*

CHAPTER ...ONE

If it were up to Zac, the Power family would have stayed right where they were, cruising in a jumbo jet 30,000 feet above the ocean.

Zac sat listening to his iPod with the sound turned right up, finishing off his chocolate ice-cream. The cabin was dark. Around him, everyone was dozing. It was as warm and cosy as naptime at kindergarten.

'Zac! Take off those headphones this minute and listen to me.'

His mum's cross face appeared beside him in the darkness. She showed him the time on her chunky digital wristwatch.

Uh oh.

'You were supposed to have your gear on three minutes ago,' his mum said, half-whispering and half-yelling. 'We can't afford mistakes at this stage of the mission, Zac.'

Sighing, Zac reached under the seat for his backpack. He'd been having an excellent daydream about playing a guitar solo in front of thousands of fans. But there was no chance he'd be doing that any time soon.

Instead, Zac slipped on his jumpsuit, goggles and parachute.

Zac looked over at his brother, Leon. Leon was already changed and was busy tucking his favourite book, The Manual of Advanced Electronic Gadgets (4th Edition), safely into his jumpsuit pocket.

Again Zac wondered how he'd ended up with a big brother as geeky as Leon.

Zac's dad leaned over from the seat behind them.

'Nervous, Leon?' his dad asked.

Leon was shaking with fear already.

'What about you, Zac?' his dad asked.

As if he was worried! He was 12 years old now, and anyway, he'd done this kind of thing a million times before.

If anything, Zac was bored. What was the point of death-defying adventures if you had to keep them secret? His mates had no idea Zac was a spy for the Government Investigation Bureau (or GIB for short).

Agent / ZAC POWER
SPY NAME / AGENT ROCK STAR
AGE / 12
SCAN HERE >>>

IDENTITY TOP SECRET

GOVERNMENT
G I B
INVESTIGATION BUREAU

As far as they knew, Zac was away on another soppy old family holiday. There was nothing cool about that.

Anger bubbled up in Zac. He was just about to say something to his dad when he noticed an air hostess walking towards him. She had a fake-looking smile on her face.

'Would you like a lolly, little boy?' she asked.

Little boy! Zac's fists clenched.

'Come with me,' she went on, 'and I'll show you where they are.'

The air hostess pushed Zac towards the back of the plane and through some curtains. A bowl of lollies sat on the bench. Zac took a red one, but the air hostess slapped it out of his hand.

'No! The green one,' she said, sounding tough now that they were alone.

Zac popped the green lolly into his mouth. The sugar coating melted instantly, leaving behind a small disc on his tongue.

'Your mission,' explained the air hostess. 'Guard it carefully.'

Then she stepped on a square of carpet and a trapdoor popped open.

'Into the airlock,' she ordered.

Zac stepped down into the dark space beneath the trapdoor. He straightened his goggles and ran his fingers through his dark brown hair. It flopped back into exactly the same place, the way it always did.

He was ready. The air hostess silently counted down on her fingers.

...5
...4
...3
...2
...1
–

Zac took a flying leap out of the airlock and into the black night.

A split-second later, Zac was falling at 200 kilometres an hour. Wind rushed past him. It roared in his ears. It sucked his cheeks back hard against his skull.

Zac tugged his ripcord and his parachute opened.

WHOOF!

His whole body jolted as he slowed to a drift.

Finally, Zac's sneakers slammed into the ground below. He'd found the drop zone. He fell clear of his chute and into a commando roll.

He got up and looked around. Where on earth was he? He didn't know what dangers would be waiting for him, or what kind of people he might meet on this mission.

Whoever they were, one thing was for sure – they wouldn't be looking forward to a friendly visit from Zac Power.

CHAPTER ...TWO

It was hot, steamy and very, very dark. Zac held his hand up in front of his face. Nothing. He couldn't see even a centimetre in front of him.

The darkness made the croaking of frogs and the angry buzzing of insects seem even louder. It was raining hard, and Zac was soaked already.

He felt in his pocket for his SpyPad.

The SpyPad looked a bit like an electronic game, but was actually a mini-computer, mobile satellite telephone with voice scrambler, laser and code breaker all rolled into one.

Zac had the turbo deluxe model, which came with colour screen and true tone sound effects for the in-built games. But this was no time for games.

Zac spat out the disc the air hostess had given him and loaded it into his SpyPad.

...Loading...

CLASSIFIED

MISSION RECEIVED
SUNDAY 11.59PM

The evil Dr Drastic has invented
something called Solution X.
This is a cure for every type of
disease that has ever existed.

Sources tell us that Dr Drastic
is making Solution X in a top-secret
laboratory somewhere
on Poison Island.

YOUR MISSION
· Find the secret lab.
· Secure the formula for Solution X.
· Return it safely to Mission Control
before Monday 12.00am.

END

STUN GUN
>>> OFF

Suddenly, Zac heard a noise behind him.

THUNK!

He turned around.

Then he heard it again.

THUNK!
THUNK!

Somewhere to his right, Zac heard foot-steps. A hand clapped him across the back.

'Rough landing, son?' his dad asked. 'That was Agent Frost playing the air hostess. Hopeless, didn't you think?'

Nothing about spying was ever easy or comfortable, in Zac's experience. He wished they could just get on with the mission. Then he could get home and practise more Green Day songs.

His mum's serious voice cut through his thoughts like a knife.

'What are our orders, Zac?'

As Zac passed her the SpyPad, he heard a worried voice. 'Mum? Dad? Zac?'

'Shhh, Leon! Anybody could be listening,' said his mum, as she read the orders from Zac's SpyPad.

'Right. It's 1.21am. That doesn't give us much time. I suggest we separate,' said his dad.

Zac's mum consulted her wristwatch

compass. 'OK, Zac, you and Leon head east to the centre of the island.' Then she added in a quiet voice just for Zac, 'I'm counting on you to look after Leon.'

Zac rolled his eyes. His mum may as well have put handcuffs on him. Even though he was older, Leon was slow, scared and a generally hopeless spy. Zac wished, just this once, he could finish a mission all by himself.

He'd *really* be a hero then.

'Your mum and I will search the coastline,' his dad continued. 'If you see anything suspicious, message us with your SpyPad.'

As his parents left, Zac's mum whispered in his ear. 'We're heading straight home after the mission. You've got to walk Espy.' Espy, short for Espionage, was the family dog.

With that, his parents were gone. Zac and Leon were alone.

'Ready, Leon?' asked Zac gruffly.

'Um, Zac…I'm tangled in my parachute.'

Zac sighed. It was going to be a very long mission.

Zac and Leon might have been walking through the jungle, but it felt like they were swimming in glue. Zac was hot and tired already, and they'd only been walking for an hour.

Dripping with sweat, Zac stopped to listen for the crunch of Leon's footsteps. But behind him, everything was silent. *Surely not even Leon could be lost already?*

Zac turned. There was Leon, a few steps back. He was standing with his head to one side, listening to something. His glasses were two round patches of steam.

'Listen, Zac,' he whispered, out of breath.

'Who is it? Dr Drastic?'

'No,' said Leon. 'Frogs.'

Zac gave Leon his 'Like I Care' face.

'Hundreds of them,' Leon continued.

'And by the sounds of it, they're dentrobates!'

Zac grabbed Leon's arm. He almost ripped it from the socket.

'Let's just keep moving, OK?'

'Dentrobates, or Poison Dart Frogs,' said Leon in a huff, 'have the most deadly poison of any known animal in the world.

DENTROBATE

a.k.a
POISON DART FROG

DANGER!
Skin contains
a deadly poison.

DO NOT TOUCH!

Poisonous Skin

BEWARE

If you just *touch* one it will paralyse or even kill you.'

'Right. Whatever,' said Zac, pretending he wasn't impressed.

They walked on in silence.

A few minutes later, something made Zac stop again. He had the creepy feeling that someone was watching them.

Then Zac heard a noise – it was so quiet he wasn't sure it was real.

There it was again! It sounded like leaves rustling. He hadn't imagined it.

Next, Zac heard a click and the soft whistling sound of something flying through the air.

'Did you hear that, Leon?' he whispered.

Silence.

'Leon?' he said again. 'Are you OK?'

But Leon didn't answer. When Zac turned to look at him, Leon had the weirdest look on his face, like he was sleeping with his eyes open.

Leon wobbled unsteadily on his feet. He was going to collapse!

Zac saw something sticking out of Leon's back. A dart! That was what he'd heard whistling through the air.

Zac ran back. He braced himself for a **WHOOMP!** as his brother hit the ground.

But suddenly a huge net fell from the trees above. Leon was tangled up like an insect in a spider's web. Pulleys dragged the net up into the treetops again, taking Leon with them.

It was a booby trap! And the men firing the darts must be Dr Drastic's henchmen. Was Leon dead or alive? Zac couldn't tell.

Zac's stomach twisted in knots. He was supposed to look after Leon, but now Dr Drastic had him. He'd failed his parents. Even worse, Zac knew he'd failed GIB. Now that Leon was captive, Dr Drastic would know that GIB agents were on the island, looking for his secret lab.

Whichever way you looked at it, Zac had blown the entire mission!

CHAPTER ... THREE

Zac had only been standing there, thinking those dreadful thoughts, for a few seconds. But it felt like hours. And it must have given Dr Drastic's henchmen the time they needed to reload their dart guns because...

Fffft!

Fffft!

Fffft!

A hail of darts shot through the darkness, straight towards Zac.

Zac knew exactly what he had to do. On his first day in spy school, Zac had learnt an important lesson:

GIB

WHATEVER HAPPENS,
A SPY MUST ALWAYS
COMPLETE THE MISSION.
THERE'S NO ROOM FOR SYMPATHY
AND NO ROOM FOR FEAR.

He'd have to rescue Leon later. Right now, Zac had to run.

Dr Drastic's henchmen were getting close.

'Sending two kids!' sneered one of them. 'GIB must be getting desperate for spies.'

Blood pounded angrily in Zac's head. *Kids! How dare they!*

He'd never moved so fast in all his life.

'Stop him!' yelled one of the henchmen. 'He's getting away!'

The two henchmen raced through the jungle after him.

In the heat and panic, voices seemed to rush at Zac from all directions. Which way was forward? Which was up? Which was down? Was he going in circles?

It didn't matter.

He just had to get as far away from those voices as he could.

Zac had no idea how far he ran, or for how long. Eventually, he noticed the voices behind him fading until, finally, they were gone. He'd outrun Dr Drastic's henchmen.

Hiding himself carefully behind a tree, Zac stopped at last. He had to decide what to do next.

He felt in the pocket of his cargo pants for his SpyPad. Yes, there it was. Safe and sound. He flicked it on.

He could call his parents, but that would mean telling them he'd lost Leon. He could call GIB, but then he'd have to admit he'd blown his cover. Zac imagined his mum's face as he told her Leon had fallen into one of Dr Drastic's booby traps.

He punched in the secret number for GIB. The phone at Mission Control rang.

'This is GIB. Prepare for security clearance.'

Zac held his SpyPad to his fingertip while it scanned his fingerprint.

'Hello, Zac,' said a voice at Mission Control.

'Oh, hi,' began Zac. 'I – aahhhhhhhhh!'

'Zac? Do you read me?' came the voice on the other end of the SpyPad.

But Zac couldn't hear it. He'd tripped on a tree root, stumbled forward and let go of his SpyPad. As if in slow motion, the SpyPad was flying through the air. It hit a pitch of sandy ground, then, mysteriously, began to sink.

Oh no! thought Zac. *Quicksand!*

A spy must never be without a SpyPad. Zac had to get it back! He jumped into the quicksand, and straight away his hands closed around the SpyPad. Yes! It was safe.

Right, thought Zac. *Now to get out of this quicksand. It can't be so hard…*

He tried to lift his left leg out. But the quicksand moved underneath him like liquid. It sucked him down even lower!

He tried his right leg.

No luck! He was sinking fast.

Zac knew the best way to get out of quicksand: stay still and wait for someone to come and pull you out. But no-one except for Dr Drastic's henchmen knew even roughly where he was.

An idea popped into Zac's head. *What if he let himself sink all the way through the quicksand until he reached solid ground at the bottom?*

Then he could use his official GIB Tramp-o-Socks to bounce his way out. Tramp-o-Socks were like ordinary sports socks, except each heel was fitted with an extra-springy miniature trampoline.

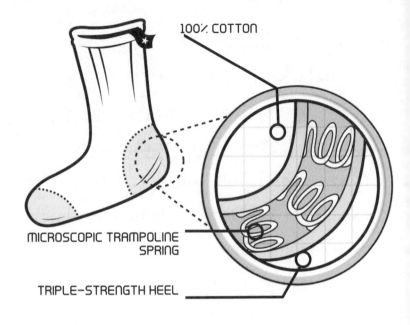

100% COTTON

MICROSCOPIC TRAMPOLINE
SPRING

TRIPLE-STRENGTH HEEL

Zac took a deep breath and duck-dived under the quicksand. It swallowed him up with a...glub...glub...glub!

Zac wiggled off one sneaker, then the other. Even the slightest effort made him feel dizzy.

He was running out of air!

But just when Zac thought he couldn't hold his breath for a second longer, he hit solid ground. With all his might, he hurled his heels in their Tramp-o-Socks against the bottom.

Zac shot up, up, up through the quicksand and burst out the top. He soared though the air, gasping for air as he flew.

THUD!

He landed heavily on solid rock.

He was right near the mouth of a cave.

CHAPTER ...FOUR

Zac crawled into the gloomy cave. Rocks cut his knees, but he didn't care. He was just too tired to stand up.

The cave smelt awful, like dead bat and sweaty armpit mixed together. Zac hardly noticed. A dark cave was the perfect place to hide for a while. Right now, that was all that mattered.

Feeling along the rocky cave walls, Zac

came to a ledge sticking out. Relieved, he crawled underneath and took out his SpyPad. The message light was blinking. Maybe someone at GIB knew he was in trouble and was sending back-up!

MESSAGE RECEIVED 8:03AM

Thieves have raided Government Mint. Millions of dollars stolen. Agent Tool Belt (dad) and I have been sent to investigate. We're sure you and Leon can handle Dr Drastic yourselves.

Remember, it's your turn to walk Espy:-)

MESSAGE FROM AGENT BUM SMACK (MUM)

MESSAGE
>>> READ MODE

Water dripped on Zac's head. He shivered. Everything now depended on him. Just a couple of hours ago, Zac had been wishing he could finish a mission all by himself. Now that it was really happening, Zac wasn't sure he liked it after all.

Zac switched his SpyPad to Message mode. He needed to send GIB a full update. He was typing away when he heard a sound.

It sounded like footsteps!

Zac crouched down lower under the rock ledge. Yes, it was definitely footsteps, and they were coming his way.

He stayed statuc-still.

He hardly dared to breathe!

'How long's this gonna take, Bruce?' said a man's voice.

Zac listened closely. The voice was the same one he'd heard back in the jungle when Leon was captured. It seemed to come from further inside the cave.

'As long as Dr Drastic says, Bradley,' said the second henchman.

What now? thought Zac.

He could make a break for it and run out of the cave. But he didn't like his chances of outrunning the henchmen twice in one day. Better to stay hidden. He might even learn something.

As though he'd read Zac's mind, Bradley piped up with a question.

'Anyway, what's Dr Drastic got in that lab that's so important?' he said.

'You fool! It's the boss's biggest ever project! Solution X,' said Bruce.

'Oh, yeah? And how's he make that?'

In his rocky hiding place, Zac went red with excitement. This knucklehead was about to give him just the clue he needed to get the mission back on track!

'Seen those poison frogs everywhere? Well, the boss discovered if you boil their poison and add a few secret ingredients, you get Solution X.'

'Wow,' said Bradley.

Zac could tell that he didn't understand anything Bruce had said.

'It's gonna make the boss rich,' said Bruce.

'So where do those little brats from GIB fit in?'

Brats! Zac wished he could shout back something really rude.

'Dr Drastic told the world's govern-ments he'll sell them Solution X if they pay one million dollars each within 24 hours. Guess they don't want to pay. GIB must've sent the kids to find the formula before time runs out and Dr Drastic destroys it,' sniffed Bruce.

Bradley sniggered. 'Do they know he's gonna kill that nerdy Leon kid too?' he asked.

Kill Leon? Zac shivered.

'Dunno, Bradley. All we have to worry about is keeping Solution X and the kid safely locked in the lab until the deadline passes,' said Bruce.

'I'm sitting down then,' said Bradley. 'Bet we'll be guarding the lab entrance for a while. And I'm starving!'

The lab must be somewhere on the other side of Bruce and Bradley! Zac had to get past them, fast. But how?

Suddenly, Zac had an idea. It was risky, but things were really desperate now.

He turned his SpyPad to Voice Scrambling mode. He took a deep breath and shouted into the microphone. 'Hot pies!

Ice-cream! Ice cold drinks!'

The voice that came out didn't sound like Zac's voice at all.

It sounded exactly like a grown man selling snacks at a footy ground.

'Awwwright!' said Bradley greedily. 'I could really go a pie right now.'

'Me too!' said Bruce. 'Didn't know there were snack vans on the island though,' he said thoughtfully.

'Me neither. First time for everything, I guess!' Bradley said.

'Hot chips!' called Zac through the

Voice Scrambler.

Bruce and Bradley stood up. They practically fell over each other to be first out of the cave.

'I'm getting a pie and chips. Or maybe two pies!' said Bruce, running.

'Reckon they'll have tomato sauce out here?' said Bradley, his voice fading into the distance.

Zac had done it! The cave was empty. Next stop – Dr Drastic's secret lab.

CHAPTER ...FIVE

By now, Zac's eyes were used to the darkness inside the cave. He saw stalactites hanging down from the roof like daggers. Directly in front of him was a long, narrow tunnel leading further into the cave. That had to be the way to the lab!

He set off along the passage. He ran, but carefully. There was a stream running along the floor of the tunnel and the rocks were slippery. He couldn't afford to fall and crack his head. Solution X and Leon would be lost for sure.

Then again, Zac didn't know how long Bruce and Bradley would wander through the jungle looking for a snack van that didn't exist. Yes, they were thick. But *how* thick?

The deeper into the cave Zac went, the narrower the tunnel became. Soon he was on all fours, only just squeezing through.

It got darker.

And colder.

And scarier.

If something happened to Zac down here, he knew he would never be found.

Just as soon as he thought this, the

rocky passage walls started to shake! Deep rumbling sounds came at him from every direction.

BOOM! BOOM! BOOM!

Rocks pelted down all around him. The passage was caving in! It was another one of Dr Drastic's booby traps. Zac must have accidentally triggered a trip wire.

Zac tried to speed-crawl forward along the tunnel. But a huge pile of rocks blocked his way. He crawled backwards along the tunnel, only to find an even bigger pile of rocks there.

Zac was trapped.

He felt around in his pockets.

He needed something – anything! – to dig with. But Zac had nothing but his SpyPad, a roll of grape Bubble Tape with hair stuck to it and his iPod.

Wait – his iPod!

His dad was always telling him he had his music up so loud it made the walls shake.

Maybe I could force the rocks out of the way by triggering another rockslide using sound waves, thought Zac.

There was always the risk that even more rocks would fall, but it was his only chance.

Zac hooked his iPod to his SpyPad.

His SpyPad had awesome built-in speakers. They were unbelievably powerful for something so small.

Zac checked the music on his iPod.

To trigger a rockslide, he'd need something really, really loud! He found the Axe Grinder's latest single, 'Torture Your Ears'.

Perfect!

Zac set the volume to ten.

He blocked his ears and hit play.

yelled Axe Grinder's singer.

The force of the sound waves blew Zac across the tunnel. There was no word for it other than awesome. But best of all, the rocks blocking Zac's way forward had been blown apart! All that stood in his way now was a big pile of dust.

Zac got back down on all fours. He crawled deeper into the tunnel. Axe Grinder's rock concert had been very cool, but there was no time to waste.

It was already 2:43pm!

He must be getting close to Dr Drastic's lab by now. And sure enough, the tunnel started to widen. The stream on the floor of the tunnel deepened. Soon Zac was standing knee-deep in water.

He rounded a final bend. The tunnel ended in an enormous, rocky chamber. Zac found himself on the edge of a lake that took up most of the area.

He took a look around. *If this is the end of the tunnel*, thought Zac, *then the entrance to the secret lab must be somewhere in this rocky room.*

But where? All Zac could see were smooth, hard walls. No secret passages. No doors with codes to crack.

Absolutely nothing.

Then, in the darkness, Zac almost

tripped over something stuck into the shore of the lake. He got down low to have a good look.

It was a sign that said 'No Fishing'. Beside the writing was a picture of a fisherman looking alarmed as a fish with huge and bloody fangs chewed his arm right off.

It was a piranha!

Zac had seen a dead one once, on a mission in the Amazon. A piranha could chew all your skin off in ten minutes flat. But what would a fish that only lives in the Amazon be doing on Poison Island?

Unless…

Suddenly, Zac was certain. *The lab entrance must be right at the bottom of the lake, protected by Dr Drastic's final booby trap!*

A piranha-infested lake!

CHAPTER SIX

In his mind, Zac made a list of things he'd need to dive into the piranha-infested lake.

First, a diving mask.

But he didn't have one.

Second, an oxygen tank. No, he didn't have one of those, either. GIB didn't think he'd need one in the middle of a jungle.

Third, a piranha-proof suit.

PIRANHAS

a.k.a KILLER FISH

TO AVOID PIRANHAS
YOU WILL REQUIRE

1 x DIVING MASK
1 x OXYGEN TANK

MOST IMPORTANT
1 x PIRANHA-
PROOF SUIT (extra
strong)

Razor sharp teeth

BEWARE

No, he'd left that at home, too.

OK, Zac, he thought. *You'll just have to dive in anyway.*

He took a confident step towards the water. He stopped. *Or maybe there's another entrance to the lab somewhere else?*

But deep inside, Zac knew there wasn't.

He took a huge breath and jumped in.

Zac swam downwards, careful not to kick too much or wave his arms around. A big splash, he knew, would only attract the piranhas. At the moment, the lake seemed still. Not a single piranha anywhere.

Although…argh!

What was that creepy, slimy thing that just brushed past him?

In a panic, Zac kicked his legs. He thrashed his arms around. He screamed inside his head, *GET THAT PIRANHA AWAY FROM ME!*

He looked left. He looked right. But all there was floating near him was a gloopy clump of seaweed.

So that's what brushed against me, thought Zac with relief. *As long as I don't make any big splashes, I'm safe.*

But even as Zac was thinking this, he realised he was still splashing around like crazy. The piranhas would find him any second! He had to swim to the bottom as fast as he could.

Down he swam at double speed.

Near the bottom, Zac saw what looked like a round door with a handle in the middle. The entrance!

Zac grabbed hold of the handle and pulled as hard as he could.

Yes! The door was heavy, but at least it was shifting. He pulled on the handle again. It was definitely coming loose! Only one more big heave and Zac would be in the lab.

Staring hard at the door, he collected every ounce of strength he had. He was just about to heave one last time when…

A piranha!

It swam right between Zac's face and the door, its mouth gaping open. It examined Zac's forearm. *Mmm, lunch!* it seemed to be thinking.

Desperately, Zac felt about for something to distract it. And there it was, in the pocket of his cargo pants. The entire roll of Bubble Tape with hair stuck to it!

Zac broke open the pack and made a

giant ball of bubble gum.

The piranha opened its terrible mouth. Its razor-sharp teeth flashed. In a second, Zac had stuffed the ball of gum into the surprised piranha's mouth.

A moment later, Zac was through the round door, through an airlock and into Dr Drastic's mysterious laboratory.

CHAPTER ... SEVEN

What Zac found on the other side of the door was just what he expected an evil science lab to look like.

Every surface gleamed white and silver. Coloured potions in glass containers bubbled and smoked over flames. Across one wall were rows and rows of tanks, all full of frogs. Each frog had a tube attached to it. Zac saw the deadly poison slowly drip,

drip, dripping up each tube and into a huge vat on the floor.

The only thing missing were the scientists. The lab was completely deserted.

Zac knew he had to work fast. He'd found one of the ingredients in Solution X – the frog poison. That was obvious. *But what were the other special ingredients mixed with the poison to create the miracle cure?*

He had to complete the formula.

Nearby, Zac saw a shelf full of books.

Zac wasn't normally that into books. But today he was. A book was just the place a complicated formula might be written down.

Zac raced over to the shelves.

He grabbed a book. *Family Recipes*, it said on the cover in curly gold writing. That looked promising. But on the first page, there was nothing but a whole lot of old-fashioned hand-writing with the heading, 'Mrs Drastic's World-Famous Meatloaf'.

Zac was getting impatient. He had no time for Mrs Drastic's cookbooks.

Faster and faster he searched, scanning every single book on the shelves. *101 Birthday Cakes for Evil Boys*. No good.

Tripe, Liver & Onions – A Treasury of Horrible Treats. Euch! No way!

Finally, Zac came to a book that was smaller than the rest. It had no title at all.

Perhaps…

He opened it.

This book had three formulas inside, but just like the cover, none of them had a title. Each of them listed 'Frog Poison' as the first ingredient.

Suspicious, Zac thought. *Any of these recipes could be Solution X!*

Zac checked his watch.

It was 6.36pm!

He needed to know which was the right recipe, and fast. There was only one way to find out: mix up each recipe then try them all himself.

Zac rushed over to a nearby cupboard. Sure enough, it was filled with hundreds of glass bottles, each with a weird-sounding name on the label. He grabbed a crusty mixing bowl from a sink and rinsed it out.

As quickly as he could, he threw all the ingredients from the first recipe into the bowl, mixed them together and swallowed them down.

He felt nothing. But then he saw his reflection in the bottom of a dirty saucepan. His eyes were changing colour! One minute they were pink, the next they were gold and the next they were fluoro orange.

This couldn't be the right recipe.

He mixed up the second recipe and

swallowed that too. Zac coughed. His cough sounded like a canary singing! Also not the right recipe.

Desperately, Zac mixed together the third recipe. He gulped it down and waited.

Nothing happened.

He checked his eyes in the saucepan. They were brown, as normal. He coughed. That sounded like a normal cough too.

This must be it! thought Zac.

He'd found the formula for Solution X! Suddenly, a very loud grinding sound filled the lab.

Zac spun round. The entire bookshelf was turning around — it was a revolving door. Behind the bookshelf, Zac saw a dusty tea-break room, where lab assistants sat reading magazines and drinking coffee.

And there, in the doorway, stood a pale-skinned man with cold blue eyes and an explosion of white hair on his head. He was wearing a lab coat. Zac saw a name-tag pinned to the chest.

It read: Dr Victor Drastic.

Dr Drastic stuck out his hand.

'Zac Power?' he asked.

Zac's mouth dropped open in horror.

But his tongue wasn't acting like it normally did. It unrolled and unrolled and unrolled, and at the end, a whistle blew.

The third recipe had turned Zac's tongue into a party whistle!

Zac was about to be captured. And he didn't have the formula for Solution X after all!

CHAPTER ... EIGHT

'Step this way, Mr Power,' said Dr Drastic. 'Watch your head on the revolving book-case.'

He was calm and polite, but icy. It was exactly how Zac's teachers sounded when someone tried the 'dog ate my homework' line on them.

Zac felt Dr Drastic's hands on his shoulders. His bony fingers and sharp fingernails dug in hard, like claws. Zac knew there was no running away from a grip like that.

'I knew you'd come sooner or later to save your brother,' said Dr Drastic. 'Couldn't resist trying to make yourself a hero, could you, Zac?'

Dr Drastic's cold, blue eyes locked with Zac's. There was something funny about the left one. Zac couldn't tell exactly what it was.

All of a sudden, Dr Drastic reached up and popped out his left eyeball altogether.

He laid it in his palm and showed it to Zac.

'It's glass. I lost my real eye a long time ago.'

Zac had never seen anything as gross as Dr Drastic's glass eye. Unless it was the empty socket where Dr Drastic's real eye used to be.

'Hasn't your mother ever told you it's rude to stare?' snapped Dr Drastic. 'Probably not. She's always too busy spying for GIB.'

He popped his glass eye back in and Zac sighed with relief.

'I bet you hate being a spy,' said Dr

Drastic, suddenly cunning. 'You'd much rather make yourself popular with your friends. Being a spy doesn't make you look cool because you can't tell anyone about it, can you?'

Zac nodded dumbly. How did Dr Drastic know all this stuff about him? It made him feel weak and stupid all of a sudden.

So that's what they mean by an evil genius, Zac thought.

'Well, would you like to see Leon?' said Dr Drastic. 'Not to rescue him, of course. Just to say hello.'

He sounded friendly again, as though he were asking Zac if he'd like a chocolate milkshake. His personality changed from nasty to friendly and back again every second minute.

It's scarier than him being horrible all the time, Zac thought.

Dr Drastic strode over to a large silver door on the opposite side of the lab. He flung it open and inside Zac saw Leon. But Leon wasn't standing, or even sitting with his wrists bound together with rope the way captives often are.

Instead, Leon was frozen inside an enormous block of ice. The expression frozen on Leon's face wasn't one of pain or fear. His forehead was wrinkled and he had a finger pressed to his cheek.

That's exactly how Leon looks when he's studying or concentrating very hard on something, thought Zac.

Dr Drastic slammed the freezer door shut. 'Don't fret, Zac,' said Dr Drastic, patting Zac's cheek creepily. 'I left an air bubble in the iceblock. Leon's still alive.'

Relief flooded through Zac. If Leon was still alive, there was always a chance Zac could come up with some last-minute plan and save him, and maybe the formula for Solution X, too.

Zac looked around him. All the windows and doors in the lab looked really secure. Now break-time was over, Dr Drastic's assistants were everywhere.

There was absolutely no way to escape.

Zac's spirits sank again.

'If I don't get my money, I'm going to destroy Solution X, you see,' Dr Drastic was saying. 'And while I'm at it, I thought I'd do away with Leon here, too.'

Dr Drastic walked over to a model of the island in the very centre of the lab.

'I'm going to drop them both into this volcano,' Dr Drastic said, pointing to a mountain on the model. A label stuck to the side read, 'Mount Humble'.

Zac's mind went into overdrive. He knew there was a volcano on Poison Island, but it hadn't erupted for hundreds of years.

'Ah! I see you're confused. Before you

ask, Zac — yes. You're correct. Mount Humble is an extinct volcano. Or rather, *was* an extinct volcano.'

Dr Drastic picked up a jar of powder that looked like pepper from a nearby bench.

'I call my latest invention Eruption Powder. It works like pepper on a human nose. I simply sprinkle it into the crater of the extinct volcano, triggering a kind of giant, volcanic sneeze. And when the volcano's good and hot again, I'll drop in the formula for Solution X.'

'Along with Leon,' said Zac grimly.

'Correct!' said Dr Drastic. 'And you too, now that you're here.'

He pulled a watch on a chain from the pocket of his lab coat.

There was less than an hour until the deadline expired!

'There's a car waiting to take us to Mount Humble,' said Dr Drastic, with an evil laugh. 'I'm dying to hear that giant ice-block sizzling in the hot lava, aren't you?'

CHAPTER ... NINE

Dr Drastic's ute bumped along the rough jungle track towards Mount Humble. Zac's hands and feet were tied together with vines. He was squashed between Bruce and Dr Drastic. Bradley was driving.

The giant block of ice, with Leon still frozen inside, was tied down in the back. It was late at night now, but the jungle heat was still fierce.

As sneakily as possible, Zac turned his head to get a better look at the block of ice. It seemed to be melting fast. Was it possible it might melt before they reached Mount Humble?

'Do you fancy a little car game, Zac?' asked Dr Drastic, not waiting for an answer. 'I'll start. I spy with my little eye something beginning with…S.'

'Sweat?' said Zac, looking at Bradley's stinky, sweaty armpits. The more he played along with Dr Drastic's stupid games, the more time he'd have to dream up a rescue strategy. He had to be careful, though. Dr Drastic would be expecting some kind of escape attempt.

'Good try, but no,' said Dr Drastic. 'S is for "small boy trying to figure out how to rescue his brother and save the day."'

Bruce laughed nastily and poked Zac in the ribs. Zac sighed.

'Give up, Zac. There is no escape. You won't be saving Leon. You're not getting the formula. It's O-V-E-R,' said Dr Drastic.

'That spells over,' Bruce added.

At the worst poss-ible time, Zac had really drawn a blank. He was all out of ideas!

'Look! Over there!' cried Dr Drastic. 'It's Mount Humble!'

He clapped his hands with delight.

The ute turned off the main track and started climbing steadily up the side of the volcano. Before long, the ute stopped. Dr Drastic got out and ordered Bradley to unload the block of ice with Leon inside.

Zac hopped along awkwardly. Walking wasn't easy with both feet tied together.

Bradley hauled the block of ice over to the very edge of the volcano crater. Bruce was busy sprinkling something into the crater itself. Dr Drastic watched Zac with amused eyes.

'Yes, Zac. That's my Eruption Powder Bruce is sprinkling,' said Dr Drastic in his nastiest voice. He dug out his pocket watch and consulted it. 'The volcano will erupt in five minutes, exactly when the deadline runs out.'

Five minutes!

Things were as desperate as they had ever been.

'And when the volcano erupts, I'll have Bradley push the iceblock into the lava. Then you'll follow. But since I created it, I'm going to save the pleasure of destroying Solution X for myself.'

Dr Drastic fumbled in the inside pocket of his lab coat. He pulled out a tiny jar of bright yellow liquid. 'This is the last sample of Solution X,' said Dr Drastic. 'I'm going

to destroy this, along with the formula.'

Dr Drastic waved a piece of notepaper in Zac's face.

The formula!

'It makes me sad to destroy Solution X. It's my greatest invention. A cure for any disease or sickness ever known.'

Dr Drastic sighed. 'It's utterly magnificent, wouldn't you say Zac?

But Zac wasn't listening. He was thinking about what Dr Drastic had said. A cure for any disease or sickness ever known.

Wasn't evil a kind of sickness? wondered Zac. *Was it possible that Dr Drastic's evilness might be cured by his very own invention?*

But suddenly, Zac heard a loud gasping sound. It was coming from the volcano crater!

The ground underneath him began to rumble and shake. Scalding hot steam hissed. Red-hot ash flew through the air.

Ah-choooooooo!

It was the loudest sneeze Zac had ever heard. He knew at once what was happening.

The volcano was erupting!

CHAPTER TEN

Everyone and everything anywhere near Mount Humble was trying to get away as fast as possible. Even the animals were escaping down the mountain any way they could.

But not Dr Drastic. He stood, calm and silent, on the edge of the volcano crater. He was holding up his tiny jar of Solution X. If only Zac could get hold of that jar!

If he was going to have any chance of that, first he'd need to break the vines that tied his wrists and ankles together. But with his hands tied together, there was no way Zac could reach his pocket-knife.

Just then, Zac felt something brush up against his feet. It was a rat, trying to escape the volcano. But unlike all the other animals, this rat wasn't running. It was fat and lazy and its stomach dragged along the ground.

It was just what Zac needed!

He hopped carefully towards the rat.

Go on! Chew off those vines! he willed it.

The rat might have been lazy, but it definitely wasn't stupid. It recognised food when it saw it. It bit into the vines around Zac's ankles, then his wrists. In a few quick chews, Zac was free.

Zac snuck up behind Dr Drastic, who was still standing on the very edge of the volcano. It would've been the easiest thing in the world to push him in. But remembering the mission, Zac realised he couldn't. He still had to get Dr Drastic to tell him the secret formula.

Suddenly, Dr Drastic drew his arm back. He was about to throw his jar of Solution X into the volcano!

Zac sprang forward. He took a humun -gous jump. He was like a football super-star! As if in slow motion, Zac snatched the jar as it spun through mid-air. He cracked open the top and poured the whole lot over Dr Drastic!

For a second, Dr Drastic just stood there with yellow goo dripping down his forehead. Then he spoke. His voice was nothing like the icy, terrifying voice he used before. Now he sounded friendly but slightly confused, like a grandpa woken too early from his nap.

Bruce and Bradley rushed over to help.

'What have you done to him, you moron?' asked Bruce, looking at Zac.

'No, Bruce. That's OK. Zac's my friend!' said Dr Drastic.

Bradley looked at Bruce, confused.

This made *no* sense to him. Bruce just shrugged his shoulders. If the boss said Zac was his friend, then Zac was his friend, as far as Bruce was concerned.

'Don't you know you're in terrible danger, Zac? We're standing on top of an erupting volcano!'

Solution X had worked! Zac had cured Dr Drastic's evilness.

'I know,' said Zac. 'But I can't escape until you tell me the formula for Solution X.'

'Oh, well. That's easy! To the frog poison, you simply add...' And he

rattled off a very long list of chemicals.

Zac tried his hardest to memorise it.

He thought he had it.

'And don't forget the most important ingredient, NaCl(aq),' said Dr Drastic. 'Solution X won't work without aqueous sodium chloride – good old sea water!

A jet of steam whooshed out of the volcano. Zac nodded. He couldn't stand around for one more second memorising formulas. That would have to do.

'How do we escape from here, Dr Drastic?' asked Zac.

'Take a hang-glider. They're just over there. I've got plenty of spares,' said Dr Drastic.

Zac raced over to a row of hang-gliders. Then he remembered Leon. How was he going to rescue his brother when he was still frozen solid in a block of ice?

He looked over at Leon. Leon was waving to him! On the side facing the volcano, the iceblock had melted enough to free Leon's arm.

Zac grabbed hold of the hang-glider. He took a big run up. Wind rushed under the wings. Zac was flying. **Whoosh!**

Zac circled over the volcano then swooped back down. Leon must have understood Zac's plan perfectly.

As Zac flew overhead, Leon held his free arm up as high as he could. Zac grabbed his hand. The entire iceblock lifted off the ground.

At last, Zac thought. *I've rescued Leon!*

But almost as soon as they were airborne, the hang-glider began to drop downwards.

Oh no! The block of ice was too heavy to fly!

They were falling straight towards the volcano crater!

The lower they fell, the hotter it got. They were dropping faster and faster!

Leon's feet were almost in the lava.

But just when Zac thought they would surely frizzle, the hang-glider suddenly rose again. Up and up it climbed, right out of the volcano crater.

Zac looked down. Flying so deep into the volcano had melted the iceblock completely. Leon was free and the hang-glider was light enough to fly again.

On the ground, they could just make out the tiny figure of Dr Drastic escaping Mount Humble in one of his hang-gliders. He gave Zac a friendly wave good bye.

Zac and Leon soared away, high above Poison Island. A few minutes later, they touched down on the deck of an enormous ship. It was GIB's floating Mission Control, anchored just off the coast of Poison Island.

Zac's mum and dad were waiting for them on board.

'Mission accomplished, boys?' asked his dad proudly.

'Uh huh,' said Zac, acting cool.

His mum gave him a big sloppy kiss.

'Mum!' said Zac. *How could she be so tragic?*

The floating Mission Control was linked via satellite to the mainland HQ.

'Zac, do you have the formula for Solution X?' crackled a voice through the computer screen. It was GIB's Commander-in-Chief on the line.

'I do, Commander,' he said confidently. 'It's — '

Oh no, the formula! What was it again?

Zac racked his brains. He had it! He rattled off the very long list of chemicals Dr Drastic had added to the frog poison. Then he remembered there was one last, critical ingredient.

What was it?

'Leon?' he whispered.

'Yup?' said Leon, his lips still blue from being inside the iceblock.

'I can't remember the last part of Solution X,' he admitted.

'That's OK,' said Leon. 'While I was frozen, I studied Dr Drastic as he was making the formula.'

So that explained the look of concentration Zac had noticed on Leon's frozen face! 'The last ingredient is NaCl(aq).'

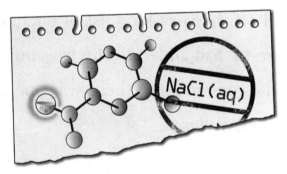

Zac was amazed.

Why hadn't he realised before how useful a geeky brother could be?

The Commander interrupted them.

'Good job, Leon. And especially well done to you, Zac,' said the Commander.

Zac tried his best to look modest.

'Of course, everything you've told us about what happened on Poison Island must remain top secret. Escaping from quicksand. The cave-in. The piranha. Everything.'

Zac slumped.

How boring!

'Just because you can't boast to your friends about it, it doesn't make what you've any done less important,' the Commander said.

Zac thought about it.

He guessed it was true.

He'd just have to get used to being an ordinary kid for a while, doing his homework and taking Espy for walks. Still, he'd have heaps of time to practise his guitar solos. Then maybe one day he'd have thousands of fans screaming his name.

Now that, thought Zac, *really would be cool*.

... THE END ...

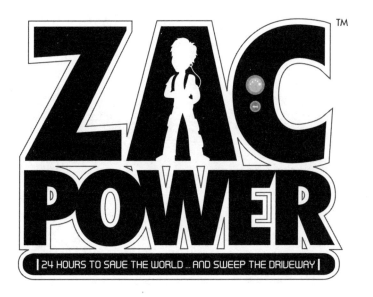

ZAC POWER™

| 24 HOURS TO SAVE THE WORLD ... AND SWEEP THE DRIVEWAY |

VOLCANIC PANIC

BY *H. I. LARRY*

ILLUSTRATIONS BY **ANDY HOOK**

CHAPTER... ...ONE

It just isn't fair, thought Zac Power as he stared at the page in front of him. *I'm a secret agent! Why am I stuck here learning fractions?*

It was almost the end of a long school day, and Zac was counting down the minutes to the bell.

He may have been a highly trained member of the Government Investigation Bureau, but that was all top secret.

As far as his school was concerned, he was just an ordinary kid.

Zac's teacher, Mrs Tran, was away that day. They had a new teacher taking their class. Usually that meant the class got to do lots of fun stuff like art and PE.

But not this time. This new teacher had made them sit at their desks all day doing maths worksheets until Zac thought his brain would melt.

The new teacher's name was Ms Sharpe. She was tall and thin, and her jet-black hair was streaked with blue.

Zac didn't like her. There was something about her smile that made Zac feel like he was in trouble, even though he was sure he hadn't done anything wrong. Not today, anyway.

Finally, the bell rang. Zac stuffed the worksheets into his maths book and got up to leave with the rest of the class.

'Just a minute please, Zac,' called Ms Sharpe. 'I need to rush off to an important meeting. Could you please close the blinds before you go?'

Zac sighed and walked back across the classroom towards the windows. He was about to pull the blinds down when suddenly, out of the corner of his eye, he saw something red and gleaming.

Sitting outside on the windowsill was a rock as big as Zac's hand, and it was glowing like it had just shot out of a volcano.

Zac looked around cautiously, but Ms Sharpe had disappeared.

His spy senses tingled. He opened the window and reached a hand out towards the rock.

For a moment, the rock burnt red hot under his fingers. But then it grew cool and turned black.

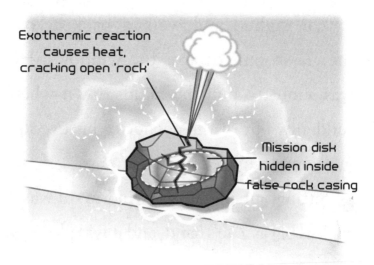

Exothermic reaction causes heat, cracking open 'rock'

Mission disk hidden inside false rock casing

A second later, the rock made a loud hissing sound and cracked open in Zac's hand, revealing a little silver disk. Zac's eyes lit up. *Excellent!*

A disk like this could mean only one thing – a new mission from GIB!

Zac smiled. His boring school day was about to get a whole lot more interesting.

CHAPTER... ...TWO

Zac raced to his schoolbag, and pulled out a small electronic device that looked a bit like a video game console.

This was Zac's new SpyPad, the Pulsetronic V-66. It did play video games, but it was also a phone, a code breaker, a laser, and just about everything else a spy could need.

Zac slipped the disk into his SpyPad.

CLASSIFIED

MESSAGE INITIATED 3:00PM
CURRENT TIME 3:33PM

GIB has received a distress
call from Agent Hot Shot, who
is stationed on a small volcanic
island called the Isle of Magma.

Agent Hot Shot reports that
the island has become extremely
active, and may erupt as soon as
tomorrow afternoon. He needs
immediate assistance.

A cloaked GIB jet is waiting for you
behind the kindergarten cubby house.

Your mission is to locate and rescue
Agent Hot Shot.

MISSION TIME REMAINING:
23 HOURS 27 MINUTES

END

Zac pulled the disk out of the SpyPad and pocketed it. Leaving his schoolbag under his chair, he dashed down the hall and raced outside.

The playground was crawling with kids and their parents. Zac knew he'd have to be careful not to let anyone see what he was doing.

He slowed down and walked the rest of the way to the cubby house at the far end of the playground.

Hang on, thought Zac as he neared the cubby house. *If the jet I'm looking for is cloaked, that means it's going to be invisible.*

How am I supposed to climb aboard a jet that I can't even see?

But Zac's question was answered a moment later when he slammed into something cold and hard. 'Ouch!'

The invisible jet was right there in front of him.

Well, Zac thought as he rubbed his throbbing head, *at least I found it.*

Now came the hard part. He had to find a way inside.

Zac stared at the empty space in front of him. He was suddenly reminded of something he'd learnt in science last term about bats using echolocation to find their way in the dark.

This gave Zac an idea. Peering around to make sure that no-one was watching, he set the laser on his SpyPad to Multi-Beam, and pointed it in the direction of the cloaked jet.

Several sharp green beams shot out of the SpyPad. The laser beam bounced off the jet in front of him, lighting it up around the edges.

Zac moved the laser across the body of the jet until he found the cockpit door.

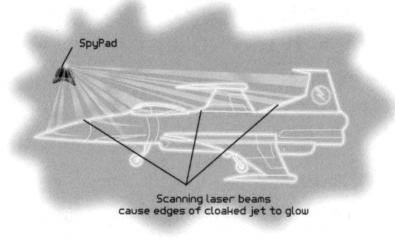

Scanning laser beams
cause edges of cloaked jet to glow

He turned off the laser, pulled on the door handle, and climbed aboard.

The cockpit of the jet was small and cramped, not at all up to GIB's usual standard. Everything inside was black, except for the gleaming blue control panel.

Before Zac had even had a chance to run a pre-flight check, the door hissed closed and the jet slowly rose into the air above the school.

Autopilot, Zac thought to himself. *Sweet!*

Zac sat back in the hard plastic seat and breathed a sigh of relief. He was finally on his way!

Even though his jet was speeding

through the air, Zac knew that the trip to the Isle of Magma would probably take several hours. It wasn't long before he started getting bored.

At first, it had been kind of cool to watch the city down below. But Zac had been on heaps of jet flights before, and he got tired of sightseeing pretty quickly. Anyway, he was out over the open ocean now, and it was getting dark, so there wasn't a whole lot to see. For a while Zac passed the time playing games on his SpyPad, but after his tenth round of *Ninja Nightmare* even that got boring.

Zac glanced at his watch again, feeling impatient.

He wished that something would happen, just to break the boredom.

And at that moment, something did.

A face appeared on the screen of his SpyPad. It was Zac's older brother, Leon.

Like the rest of the Power family, Leon worked for GIB. But Leon wasn't a field agent like Zac.

He worked on GIB technology, and was in charge of some of the cool spy gadgets that Zac and the other GIB agents used to complete their missions.

'Zac, where are you?' Leon demanded. 'You're in big trouble with mum for not having swept the leaves up from the driveway. And it's already past your bedtime!'

'Where do you think I am?' said Zac, surprised. 'I'm on a mission!'

On the screen of the SpyPad, Zac noticed Leon's raised eyebrow. 'Mission? What mission?'

'The mission to rescue Agent Hot Shot from the Isle of Magma!' said Zac. He was starting to get annoyed. 'The mission you sent me on with the cloaked jet!'

'Zac, what are you talking about?' Leon asked. 'You haven't been sent on a mission. Nothing's come through from HQ all day.'

'But I found a disk at school and...' Zac trailed off as he realised what must have happened.

'The mission disk!' Zac cried, pulling the little silver disk out of his pocket. 'It's a fake!'

Now Leon looked worried. 'Zac, you've got to turn that jet around right now and come home.'

'Right,' said Zac quickly. He reached out and started tapping at the sea of blue buttons in front of him.

Nothing happened.

'I'm locked out,' Zac said, trying not to panic. 'Nothing's working! The whole control panel is locked.'

'OK, calm down,' said Leon. He didn't sound that calm himself. 'Just, um, sit tight for a minute. I'll see what I can do from here.'

On the SpyPad's screen, Zac could see his older brother tapping frantically at his keyboard. Leon was trying to over-ride the jet's computer.

Suddenly the image of Leon on the SpyPad began to flicker.

'Leon,' said Zac, 'you're breaking up!'

'I know,' said Leon, his fingers still

flying across the keyboard in front of him.
'It looks like someone's trying to jam our
signal. I think —'

But the screen blinked and flicked off.
Leon was gone.

Zac pulled the handle of the cockpit door, but it was sealed shut.

Wherever this jet was headed, Zac Power was going with it.

And there was nothing he could do about it.

CHAPTER... ...THREE

I've got to get out of this jet! thought Zac, as he looked around for something to help him escape.

If this had been a real mission, Leon would have given him a bunch of cool new gadgets to get him out of every sticky situation. But now all he had were the contents of his pockets.

PARAGUM
BUBBLEGUM
Gives you a lift when you need it!
Net Weight minus 50kg

He had
two sticks
of ParaGum,
but even if he could open
the door, what good would it do to
parachute down into the freezing ocean?
He also had a couple of Flare Marbles, but
right now a flash of blinding light would
only make things worse.

And then of course he was wearing
his Turbo Boots, which would have been
great...except that he hadn't refuelled
them all week. They probably only had one
good jump left in them.

At least Zac wouldn't have to wait long
to find out where he was going. Looking

up, he spotted something red and glowing ahead.

It was the mouth of a volcano. An extremely *active* volcano. And he was headed straight for it.

As the jet flew closer, Zac saw that the volcano sat in the middle of a tiny tropical island. The whole place looked completely deserted.

The jet whooshed to a stop, hovering just above the mouth of the volcano. Lava splattered upwards and lashed the jet on all sides.

After a few moments, a loud siren sounded and the jet began moving again.

Zac's heart skipped a beat. The jet was

dropping. He was being flown down inside the volcano!

As the jet descended, Zac decided that he'd better be ready for anything. He pocketed the ParaGum and the Flare Marbles. Then he used the fake mission disk to back up the contents of his SpyPad, and slipped it inside his left sock.

Zac checked the time.

The jet plunged lower and lower, past brown rock and flowing lava, until it finally emerged into an enormous rocky cavern.

Zac blinked as he took in the sight. The cavern was filled with row after row of small black jets, at least fifty of them.

They were all identical to the one that Zac was sitting in.

BIG MINI-JET

That means there are lots of people down here, he thought.

Looking down, Zac saw streams of

glowing red lava criss-crossing along the floor of the cavern, in between the black jets. The lava flowed through archways that had been dug out of the rock walls.

From where Zac was sitting, it looked like his jet was being lowered down into an enormous glowing spider web.

With a jolt, Zac's jet set down between two others. Steel hooks rose up from the ground and locked around the undercarriage.

The cockpit door hissed open, and a wave of cool air washed over him.

Hang on, thought Zac. *Why is it so cold in here?* He was no scientist, but he was pretty sure volcanoes were supposed to be hot.

Zac jumped down to the floor. The cavern was eerily quiet, and his footsteps echoed loudly off the stone walls.

Then, in the distance, Zac heard the sound of hissing steam and whirring motors.

The sounds grew louder and louder until, finally, a line of three black vehicles whizzed through a tall stone archway.

The vehicles looked a bit like jet skis, but they were gliding down one of the lava channels on cushions of steam. A stream of icy water shot out of the back of each vehicle, propelling it forward.

The lava skis pulled to a stop, and two enormous women strode towards Zac out

Motorcycle-style steering

High pressure steam jets allow Lava Ski to float over lava

Liquid nitrogen-cooled water tanks

Ice-water jet thruster

Steam layer 20 to 30 cm thick

Molten lava Temperature approx. 1170°C

CLASSIFIED

BIG LAVA SKI

of the steam clouds. Both of them were dressed in matching black jumpsuits with a small lightning-bolt crest on the front.

Then a third woman stepped forward, wearing the same black uniform. She tossed back her shiny black hair.

Zac gasped. It was the substitute teacher, Ms Sharpe.

'Ah,' said Ms Sharpe with a cold smile. 'Zac Power. Welcome to BIG Central Command!'

CHAPTER... ...FOUR

Zac stared at her. He'd heard of awful teachers, but this was ridiculous.

Ms Sharpe, a BIG spy?

BIG spies were the most evil in the business. They were GIB's greatest enemies.

It seemed like every week there was some crazy new BIG plot for Zac to deal with. And now here he was at their Central Command.

'So,' Zac said, putting on a brave face, 'this was the important meeting you had to rush off to?'

'Glad you could make it,' said Ms Sharpe with a smile. She gestured towards the two women standing beside her. 'Allow me to introduce my fellow BIG agents, Hunt and Sloane.'

She clicked her fingers and the two women advanced on Zac.

BIG is right, thought Zac. These women were gigantic! If not for their uniforms, they might have been mistaken for a pair of gorillas.

Zac tried to dodge, but the big women were surprisingly quick. Hunt grabbed

Zac around the shoulders, while Sloane snatched the SpyPad from his hand and tossed it to Ms Sharpe.

'Thank you, Sloane,' said Ms Sharpe, pocketing the SpyPad. 'We can't have our hostage calling for backup now, can we?

'Now then,' she continued, 'I suppose you've already figured out why we've brought you here, smart boy that you are.'

'If you think I'm ever going to join you…' Zac began angrily, but Ms Sharpe cut him off with a cold laugh.

'No, no, boy. We're not interested in you at all. What we want is money, and lots of it.'

'Oh, right,' said Zac. 'The usual.'

'Yes, Agent Rock Star, the usual,' Ms Sharpe said. 'World domination is a costly business, and I'm sorry to say that you have done a fine job of thwarting all of our past efforts to lay our hands on GIB's money.'

'Yeah,' said Zac, 'I have, haven't I?'

'Indeed,' said Ms Sharpe. 'But not this time.'

'Oh yeah?' said Zac. 'What's so different about this time?'

'This time,' Ms Sharpe said coolly, 'you are the one we're holding to ransom. That's why I've sent my daughter to deliver a message to your agency's headquarters. Either GIB delivers 15 million dollars to us by midnight tonight, or they never see their favourite agent again.'

Zac's eyes dropped to his watch.

That left him less than two hours to get out of here!

But my mission isn't supposed to finish until tomorrow afternoon, he thought angrily. Then again, he should have known BIG would pull something like this.

'Wait a minute,' said Zac, playing for time. 'Did you say your *daughter*?'

'That's right,' said Ms Sharpe. 'Come to think of it, I believe you've met my darling daughter Caz before.'

Of course, groaned Zac.

Caz was another dangerous BIG agent. Zac had met her several times. She'd left him stranded inside a collapsing pyramid, had tried to brainwash him, and had even had a crack at infiltrating GIB Headquarters.

'Yes, my dear Caz gathered all kinds of information for me while she was working undercover at GIB,' said Ms Sharpe, 'including the designs for your mission disks.'

So that's how they made the fake disk, Zac realised.

It was time to make a move. Without a second's warning, Zac twisted under Hunt's grip and slipped a hand into his pocket. Closing his eyes tight, he pulled out a Flare Marble and threw it to the ground.

The marble shattered, sending out a flash of blinding light.

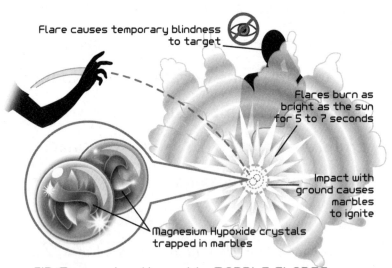

Flare causes temporary blindness to target

Flares burn as bright as the sun for 5 to 7 seconds

Impact with ground causes marbles to ignite

Magnesium Hypoxide crystals trapped in marbles

GIB Magnesium Hypoxide MARBLE FLARES

'Argh!' shouted Hunt.

Zac felt her hands loosen their grip, and he wrenched himself free.

Opening his eyes, Zac saw that all three BIG agents had been blinded by the flare.

They were now staggering around, blinking madly and snatching at the air in front of them.

Zac sprinted across the cavern in the direction of the lava skis.

'He's getting away!' yelled Sloane. 'After him!'

'Fool!' came Ms Sharpe's reply. 'You can't even see! You'll run straight into the lava! Let the boy run, he's got nowhere to go.'

Zac leapt onto one of the lava skis, brought it around and with a burst of steam, shot through the nearest archway and out of the cavern.

CHAPTER... ...FIVE

Zac zoomed on the lava ski down the channel of molten rock. He knew he needed a way to contact GIB for help.

More archways rushed by on his left and right, each one opening up into another cavern.

But every room was crawling with more BIG spies. There were hundreds of them, sitting at computers, watching surveillance screens, testing gadget prototypes.

As long as he was hidden by the cloud of steam from the lava ski, Zac thought he was probably pretty safe. But he couldn't just keep on riding up and down the corridors forever.

What I need, Zac decided, *is a disguise.*

He continued cruising down the lava stream, his eyes peeled.

Then he saw it – a little archway coming up on his right, with a sign above that read LAUNDRY.

At that moment, as Zac glanced down at the controls of the lava ski, a slight problem occurred to him.

Where on earth are the brakes?

The laundry room was coming up too fast!

Zac took a deep breath, and jumped off the lava ski, landing on a narrow stone ledge.

Up ahead, the unmanned lava ski flew out of control and smashed up into the side of the corridor, shattering a big glass pipeline that ran along the rock wall.

KER-SMASH!

Oops! thought Zac, as a torrent of water burst out from the shattered pipe. Panicked shouts echoed out from rooms nearby.

Zac ducked through the archway into the laundry room and held his breath.

'It must be Rock Star!' called a woman from down the corridor. 'He's escaped – Sharpe just sent out an alert! Quickly, this way!'

Moments later, half a dozen BIG spies ran past the laundry room archway and down the corridor.

When they were gone, Zac breathed a sigh of relief.

Digging through a nearby laundry basket, Zac found a BIG jumpsuit that was about his size.

Judging by the smell of it, Zac was half convinced that this one had been owned by something big and stinky, but there wasn't a whole lot of choice.

Zac slipped the suit on over his own clothes, and headed out into the hall.

After about twenty minutes of wandering the walkways, his eyes down to avoid attention, Zac heard a weird chugging sound coming from a room up ahead.

Looking around to make sure the coast was clear, he slipped inside to investigate.

The noise turned out to be coming from a big, bulbous pumping machine that looked like a giant mechanical spider. Huge glass pipes stretched out from each side of the machine. The pipes ran along the walls and back out the archway.

I must have smashed one of those pipes with the lava ski, Zac thought.

As Zac watched, the machine sucked up streams of brown, steaming water from the four pipes on the left, and then pumped clear, icy water out through the four pipes on the right.

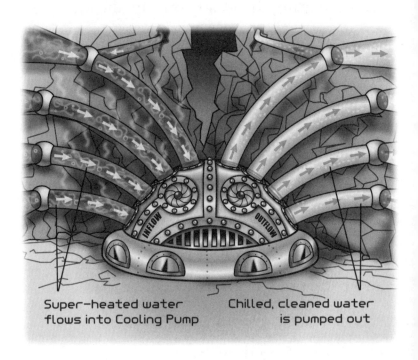

Super-heated water flows into Cooling Pump

Chilled, cleaned water is pumped out

So the pipes run through this whole place, thought Zac. *And all that cold water must be what keeps this place from burning up.*

Zac glanced around the rest of the empty room and finally found what he was looking for – a deserted computer workstation.

He reached down into his sock and pulled out the disk that he had stashed there earlier.

Slotting the disk into the computer, Zac uploaded his SpyPad's communication software. His hands fumbled with the unfamiliar keyboard, trying to get the keys to work.

At last, the screen flickered and Leon's face appeared.

'Leon!' Zac hissed, keeping his voice low. 'I need your help. I'm at BIG Central Command and –'

'I know,' Leon interrupted. 'We got the ransom note about an hour ago. We've got a team working on tracking you down. But Zac, this is huge! BIG Central Command! GIB has been trying to find that place for years!'

Zac looked at his watch.

'Yes, yes, it's all very exciting,' he said impatiently, 'but right now I wouldn't mind a hand escaping!'

'Right,' said Leon, and Zac could see him tapping on his keyboard. 'Hang on a minute, I might be able to use your connection to interface with the BIG network.'

'OK, cool,' said Zac, glancing back over his shoulder.

There was still no-one coming, but he probably didn't have much time.

'Wow,' said Leon, his eyes lighting up, 'this is an incredible system! I've never seen network security this advanced before! The encryption protocols they've put in place here are really —'

'Not now, Leon!' said Zac. Only his brother could get excited about computer security at a time like this.

'Right,' said Leon. 'Working on it.'

A second later, there was an electrical crackling. Then the lights in the room dimmed.

'Leon, was that you?'

'Yeah,' said Leon. 'At least, I think it was. I've sent through a virus to knock out the security cameras and the phone lines. That should keep you safe for a while. Now all you have to do is – whoa!'

'What?' said Zac.

'Nothing,' said Leon quickly.

'Leon!'

'Really, it's nothing,' said Leon. 'It's just that the volcano you're in is very… active.'

'I know,' said Zac. 'It was spitting lava when I got here.'

'That was nothing,' said Leon. 'BIG has set up a massive wall of electricity at the base of the volcano. Right now, that force field is holding back the worst of the lava flow. But if anything went wrong with the force field, the eruption would probably –'

'Blow the whole island apart!' Zac finished for him, a plan forming in his mind. 'Excellent!'

'What?' said Leon, sounding alarmed. 'Zac, no! It's too dangerous!'

But Leon was suddenly drowned out by a shout and the sound of approaching footsteps.

'Got to go!' said Zac, pulling his disk from the computer. The screen flickered out, just as Ms Sharpe and her bodyguards appeared in the doorway.

CHAPTER... ...SIX

'Hi,' said Zac, standing up. 'I was just leaving.'

'Oh, no you weren't,' said Ms Sharpe.

Hunt and Sloane lunged forward, but this time Zac was ready for them. He dived quickly to the ground, ducking under Sloane's legs.

Zac rolled across the floor and got to

his feet again, reaching into his pocket and pulling out a stick of ParaGum. It seemed a shame to waste it like this, instead of floating away with it, but if his plan worked…

The enormous women hovered around Zac. But he stood his ground, chewing frantically. As they drew nearer, Zac started blowing.

'Chewing gum, Agent Power?' said Ms Sharpe, raising an eyebrow as Zac's bubble grew bigger and bigger. 'I've heard of staying cool under pressure, but this is –'

BANG!!

'Argh!' cried Hunt and Sloane together as the ParaGum bubble exploded across their faces.

Zac grinned, weaved his way around Ms Sharpe and ran out of the room. For the second time that night, Sharpe's goons were left staggering behind, rubbing blindly at their eyes.

Zac raced down the corridor, hard rock on one side, bubbling lava on the other, and Ms Sharpe hot on his heels.

They were heading deeper into the facility now. Instead of laboratories and computer workstations, Zac saw that the stone archways they were passing led into smaller rooms with beds, bookshelves and small black teddy bears.

Zac glanced over his shoulder as he sprinted around another corner. Ms Sharpe was gaining on him, a steely look in her eyes.

Looking up ahead again, Zac saw a big metal door coming up on his right.

Was it unlocked? Would he be able to open it?

Zac stopped at the door and wrenched frantically at its cold metal handle.

Come on, come on…Yes!

It took both arms to heave the door open. Zac dived inside and slammed the door shut behind him with an enormous crash of metal on metal. Then he threw down the deadlock.

He heard Ms Sharpe hammering furiously on the other side of the door, but she wasn't getting through in a hurry.

I'm safe for now, he thought, glancing at his watch.

Zac had a look around the bedroom. *The bad news,* he thought to himself, *is that there doesn't seem to be another way out of here.*

Ms Sharpe had given up banging on the door, but all that meant was that she had gone for help.

He turned and looked around at the room he'd locked himself into. It was another bedroom, but this one was much nicer than the others he had just been running past.

There was an expensive-looking rug on the floor, a huge canopy bed at one end, and a wooden writing desk at the other.

Zac didn't have to look far to find out whose room he was in. There was an ID card and a little photo frame on the desk.

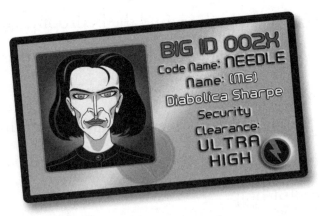

BIG ID 002X
Code Name: NEEDLE
Name: (Ms)
Diabolica Sharpe
Security
Clearance:
ULTRA
HIGH

Smiling up at him from the picture frame were Ms Sharpe and her daughter, Caz.

They were sitting on a park bench, eating ice-creams like a perfectly normal, non-evil mother and daughter.

Still, thought Zac, *there's something really creepy about that picture.*

'Zac! Hey, Zac!'

He jumped and spun around. *Where is that voice coming from?*

'Zac! Over here!'

Zac crossed over to the other side of the room, and then he saw it. Sitting on the end of Ms Sharpe's bed, blending in almost perfectly with the bedspread, was a shiny black iPod.

And it was talking to him.

CHAPTER... ...SEVEN

You've had a long day, Zac told himself sternly. *You've had a long, hard day, and now you're tired and you're imagining things. You know you're imagining things, because iPods can't talk.*

'Are you there, Zac?' said the voice.

'I know iPods can't talk!' Zac snapped.

And now you're arguing with a music player, thought Zac. *Fantastic.*

'What?' said the voice. 'Oh, right. No. Zac, it's me – Leon.'

'But –'

'Hold on a minute,' interrupted Leon, and a moment later his face appeared on the iPod screen.

'There we go.'

'Oh,' said Zac, finally catching on. 'But hold on. How are you doing that?'

'All the technology here is on a wireless network,' said Leon proudly. 'Even the iPods have been upgraded. Now that I've hacked into the system, I can pretty much go wherever I want.'

Zac grinned. For a nerd, Leon was pretty cool.

Are you there, Zac?

Press A + B = blades

Press A + C = Sleep

A + B + C = COOL AIR

Secret buttons (A), (B) and (C)

Pressing secret buttons turns iPod into a spring blade, a sleep-gas sprayer, or a 10-speed cooling fan.

BIG CUSTOMISED IPOD

'Anyway,' Leon continued, 'I tracked the path of that jet you came in on, and used it to plot a course for the back-up team to come and rescue you. They're coming out in the Squid.'

'In the what?' said Zac.

'Oh, it's really cool!' said Leon excitedly. Clearly, the Squid was one of his own inventions. 'Wait until you see! Anyway, they're almost there, so all you need to do is get back out of the volcano and –'

'I can't leave yet,' said Zac. 'I still need to bring down the force field and destroy this place!'

'No, you have to get out of there!' said Leon. 'I don't like BIG any more than you do, but it's too dangerous.'

'Leon, I can do this!' said Zac, almost shouting now. 'Look, there are plenty of jets up there for everyone to get away in. No-one will get hurt. All I have to do is stop BIG from using this place for evil.'

Leon sighed. 'I can't talk you out of this, can I?'

'No,' said Zac simply, 'you can't. Now, are you going to help me find the force field or aren't you?'

'Honestly,' Leon muttered as he went to work at his keyboard, 'you're so annoying when you get like this.'

Zac just smiled to himself.

'OK,' said Leon after a few moments, 'I have good news and bad news.'

Zac sighed. *Why is there always bad news?*

'The good news,' Leon continued, 'is that you won't have to go far to find the door that goes to the force field generator.'

'Great!' said Zac. 'Where is it?'

'You're standing on it.'

Zac stared down at his feet. Then he

reached down and heaved aside the heavy rug, uncovering a little wooden trapdoor.

Well, thought Zac, *that explains why Ms Sharpe's bedroom needs a giant metal blast door.*

'Excellent!' said Zac. 'OK, what's the bad news?'

'The bad news,' said Leon, 'is that there are about 20 BIG agents on the other side of that bedroom door, and they're approximately 30 seconds away from breaking it down.'

CHAPTER... EIGHT

BANG!

Zac's ears rang as something large and heavy crashed into the other side of the big metal door, shaking it on its hinges.

Time to go, thought Zac. He slipped the iPod into his pocket and bent down to grab hold of the brass handle at the edge of the trapdoor.

BANG!!

The whole room shook as Ms Sharpe and the other BIG agents took another shot at the door.

Zac tugged at the handle and the trapdoor lifted up easily, revealing a narrow, pitch-black tunnel. He bent down to peer inside, but couldn't see a thing.

BANG!!!

Zac looked back over his shoulder. The door was beginning to buckle.

Ms Sharpe's voice rang out from the other side of the door. 'Almost in!'

I'm almost out, Zac thought to himself, pulling a Flare Marble from his pocket. He tossed the marble down through the opening in the floor, and a moment later the whole tunnel burst into light. Careful not to look directly at the flare, Zac could see a series of thin metal bars forming a ladder down into the tunnel.

He tested the top rung with his foot and began to climb down.

No sooner had Zac's head and shoulders bobbed down into the tunnel than –

BANG!!!!

KER-SMASH!

The giant metal door exploded out of its frame and came crashing down on top of the tunnel entrance.

'Told you,' said a small voice from Zac's pocket.

Zac kept climbing down, and soon he'd reached the bottom of the tunnel. Shielding his eyes from the Flare Marble still burning at his feet, he peered around.

Now where do I go?

He didn't have to look far. From the end of a tunnel to his right, Zac heard a distant crackle of electricity. He could also see bright flashes of red, blue and purple.

Zac raced down the narrow tunnel, which turned out to be much longer than it looked.

As he drew closer to the force field generator, the fierce electrical crackling grew louder and louder until it was almost deafening.

Finally, Zac emerged from the passage-way into what turned out to be another enormous cavern, almost as big as the jet hangar at the volcano's entrance.

Zac's stomach plummeted as he looked up at the far wall of the cavern, and saw that it wasn't a wall at all. It was a surging sea of molten rock that extended for 50 metres in each direction.

The only thing stopping all that lava from spewing out and flooding BIG HQ was the paper-thin force field being projected across the cavern by a little generator in the corner. It was freaky. It was kind of like standing in front of one of those enormous shark tanks at the aquarium.

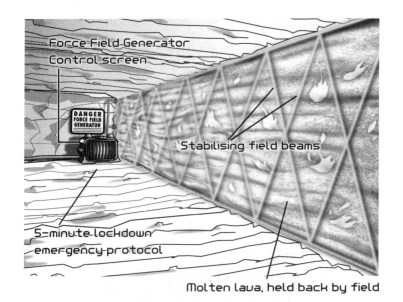

Force Field Generator
Control screen

DANGER FORCE FIELD GENERATOR

Stabilising field beams

5-minute lockdown emergency protocol

Molten lava, held back by field

And here I am, about to break the tank's glass, Zac thought.

He glanced down at his watch.

MISSION TIME LEFT 00 : 06 : 43
···G**I**B··· HRS MINS SECS
11:53:17 PM TUES

Not that the ransom deadline would matter if his plan worked.

Zac moved across the cavern to the computer station. A giant red and white sign was posted on the wall above it.

DANGER
FORCE FIELD GENERATOR

NO ACCESS.

This generator operates under a 5-minute emergency lock-down protocol. In case of emergency, agents will have 5 MINUTES to leave BIG Central Command.

Zac glanced down at the little touch screen on the side of the generator, then pulled the iPod out of his pocket.

'Leon!' he said. 'The generator is password protected! I need a code to shut it down!'

'Right,' replied Leon. 'I'm on it.'

But at that moment, Ms Sharpe burst into the room.

Zac spun around and peered down the passageway behind her. 'Where's Hunt and Sloane this time?'

'Luckily for you, they were too, er, *big* to fit through the tunnel,' Ms Sharpe said.

I bet they were, thought Zac.

'Well, you'd better head back up there

yourself,' he said. 'In a few minutes, it's going to get pretty hot in here.'

Ms Sharpe laughed. 'I don't think so, Agent Rock Star. That generator is protected by state-of-the-art BIG security. There's not a spy in the world who could shut it down.'

DING!

A large blue button appeared on the touch screen and an electronic female voice could be heard over the crackling force field.

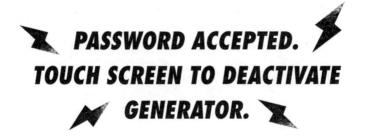

PASSWORD ACCEPTED. TOUCH SCREEN TO DEACTIVATE GENERATOR.

'Not a spy in the world,' said Zac proudly, 'except for my brother.'

Ms Sharpe looked like she'd just been punched in the stomach.

'Zac,' she said, sounding panicked, 'please, be reasonable! Let's talk about this like civilised people!'

'Right,' said Zac dryly, 'like civilised people who kidnap each other and trap them inside a volcano. I don't think so.'

He thrust out his hand toward the touch screen.

'WAIT!' cried Ms Sharpe.

Zac's finger froze, millimetres from the blue button.

'What?'

'Your grandfather!' Ms Sharpe said desperately, a mad gleam in her eye. 'I know you'd love to find him! I can help you. Come with me, Zac, and we'll find him together!'

For a long moment, the two agents stared at each other in silence. Zac's grandpa had disappeared on a jungle mission many years ago. Zac and his family had never heard from him since.

Then Zac broke the silence. 'My grandfather spent his life putting people like you out of business!'

And with that, he lifted his hand and slammed it down onto the touch screen.

CHAPTER... NINE

'Time to move!' said Zac, and he bolted past Ms Sharpe and back through the passageway.

WARNING: FORCE FIELD DEACTIVATION IN 5 MINUTES.

For a few seconds, Ms Sharpe stood frozen on the spot, staring at the force field. Then she turned on her heels and raced after Zac.

Reaching the end of the passageway, Zac clambered up the ladder and out into Ms Sharpe's bedroom.

Leaping over the battered metal door, he darted out of the room and back along the stony corridor.

Up ahead, BIG agents were streaming out into the corridor through the archways on either side, and sprinting off towards the jet hangar.

Zac could hear Ms Sharpe running behind him.

WARNING: FORCE FIELD DEACTIVATION IN 4 MINUTES.

Zac rounded another corner. Halfway down the corridor, he saw a lava ski lying abandoned on its side. He raced over, picked it up, and hoisted it down into the lava stream.

Hopping aboard, Zac took one last look around and saw Ms Sharpe staggering up the corridor, clearly out of breath.

WARNING: FORCE FIELD DEACTIVATION IN 3 MINUTES.

Zac sighed. Sometimes being a good guy was a pain in the butt.

'All right,' he said wearily, as Ms Sharpe caught up. 'Get on.'

'Huh?' she began. 'Why would you...?'

'Look, do you want to get out of here or not?' Zac snapped. 'Get on!'

Zac gave Ms Sharpe about three seconds

to climb onto the lava ski behind him, then he gunned the accelerator. In a flurry of steam, they raced along the lava stream towards the hangar.

The lava ski bucked and bounced beneath Zac's feet and it took every ounce of his game-playing reflexes to keep it from spinning out of control.

WARNING: FORCE FIELD DEACTIVATION IN 2 MINUTES.

'That was a really nice thing to do,' Ms Sharpe said suddenly.

'What?' said Zac absently, struggling to control the speeding vehicle.

'Sharing your lava ski with me,' said Ms Sharpe, 'was a really nice thing to do.'

Zac rolled his eyes. 'Yeah? Well, lucky for you I'm the nice type.'

Zac sped around one final corner and burst through the tall archway and out into the jet hangar.

'Jump!' yelled Zac, and he dived off the lava ski onto the stone floor. Ms Sharpe thudded to the ground next to him. A second later –

KER-SMASH!

The lava ski exploded against the cavern wall.

'Those things do have brakes, you know!' Ms Sharpe grunted.

'Right,' said Zac. 'Next time, you can be the driver and I'll be the evil kidnapper.'

Ms Sharpe moved to get up, but Zac stopped her with a look. 'I'll have my SpyPad back now,' he said, his hand out.

Ms Sharpe snarled and handed over the SpyPad.

WARNING: FORCE FIELD DEACTIVATION IN 1 MINUTE.

They leapt to their feet, looking around the enormous cavern. The same thought entered both of their heads.

Only one jet left. And there was no way both of them could fit inside.

'Take it!' said Zac.

'What?' said Ms Sharpe, as though she thought Zac was trying to lure her into some kind of trap.

'Take the jet!'

'But –'

'Ms Sharpe!' Zac shouted. 'You were a lousy substitute teacher and you're an even lousier spy! The only way you're going to make it out of here is in that jet! Now get in there before I change my mind!'

Casting him one last suspicious look, Ms Sharpe bolted across the cavern and climbed up into the jet.

The cockpit door hissed closed and the sleek black aircraft rose quickly up through the volcano towards the safety of the open sky.

'OK,' Zac muttered to himself, 'time to get out of here.'

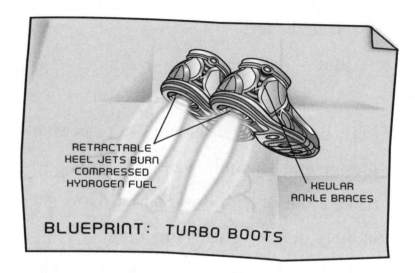

RETRACTABLE
HEEL JETS BURN
COMPRESSED
HYDROGEN FUEL

KEVLAR
ANKLE BRACES

BLUEPRINT: TURBO BOOTS

WARNING: FORCE FIELD DEACTIVATION IN TEN SECONDS.

Zac knew he had only one chance to escape.

NINE...

He ran across the floor of the cavern,

EIGHT...

leapt across the last lava stream in his path,

SEVEN...

positioned himself directly below the mouth of the volcano,

SIX...

crouched down on the ground,

FIVE...

pulled up the leg of his jeans,

FOUR...

reached for the green button on the side of his Turbo Boots,

THREE...

held his breath,

TWO...

and pushed the button.

ONE.

But absolutely nothing happened.

CHAPTER... ...TEN

That's not good, Zac thought as the whole cavern began to shake.

FORCE FIELD DEACTIVATED.

He knew his Turbo Boots were running low on fuel, but surely they had enough in them for one more jump. He pressed the button quickly with his finger.

Suddenly, lava spewed into the hangar

from all sides, gushing in through the stone archways and blasting them apart with the force. Waves of molten rock swept across the floor of the hangar, melting everything in their path.

In seconds, the whole cavern would be a swirling ocean of fire, and Zac would be at the bottom of it. The waves were only metres from him now. Only centimetres. Then –

KA-BLAM!

The twin rockets in his Turbo Boots roared to life, and he was thrown upwards.

He was tearing his way up through the throat of the volcano now, racing past the rock walls at an insane speed.

Zac looked down and saw hot lava rushing up below. The rockets in his shoes sputtered as the Turbo Boots ate up the last of their fuel.

Come on, come on! Zac thought, willing the boots to keep going. *Almost there!*

And then he was clear. Zac leant forwards and the rockets propelled him out over the ocean.

A moment later, the volcano erupted into fire and ash. *Now that,* Zac thought to himself, *was a close one.*

Then, with a final splutter, the Turbo Boots gave out and Zac began falling towards the dark sea.

Zac reached into his pocket and snatched up the last piece of ParaGum. Then he crammed it into his mouth, and chewed as hard as he could.

He was tumbling head over heels through the air now, towards the churning ocean below.

Sticking out his tongue, Zac blew into the ParaGum with all his might.

FWOOSH!

Zac's bubble was caught in an updraft and he began to drift lazily toward the water below. *Phew!*

Now where's my back-up? Zac wondered. *I thought Leon said —*

THWACK!

Suddenly, an enormous tentacle darted up from the water and caught Zac around the middle, bursting his ParaGum bubble.

'Hey!' Zac shouted out loud.

It looked like some sort of giant octopus or something, except that it was obviously mechanical.

Padded metal tentacles, like the one that had just grabbed Zac, waved in all directions, and…

Suddenly, it dawned on him.

So this is the Squid, Zac thought admiringly.

He had to hand it to his older brother. Leon certainly was creative!

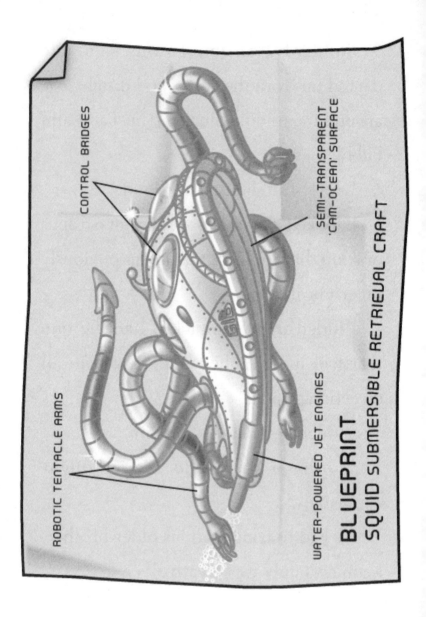

CONTROL BRIDGES

SEMI-TRANSPARENT 'CAM-OCEAN' SURFACE

ROBOTIC TENTACLE ARMS

WATER-POWERED JET ENGINES

BLUEPRINT
SQUID SUBMERSIBLE RETRIEVAL CRAFT

A hatch opened in the top of the Squid. The tentacle holding Zac lowered him inside, where Leon was waiting with the rest of the GIB back-up team.

'Need a lift?' Leon grinned.

'Yeah, thanks,' said Zac. 'Nice ride you've…'

But he trailed off when he saw his parents sitting there.

'What are you doing here?' Zac demanded, as his dad pulled him in for a hug.

'We wanted to make sure you were OK!' his mum replied. 'BIG Central Command! I never thought –'

'I told them you'd be fine,' Leon

apologised. 'But they insisted on coming as back-up.'

Zac groaned. *This is so embarrassing!*

'I'm very proud of you,' said Zac's mum, finally releasing him from a hug almost as tight as the Squid's tentacles. 'Now, let's get you home. Don't you think I've forgotten about you sweeping the driveway!'

'But…' Zac began. Surely blowing up BIG's volcano had earned him a bit of time out?

'But nothing,' his mum said sharply. 'You might have saved the world from BIG, but that doesn't mean you get out of doing your chores at home!'

'Fine,' Zac sighed. There were some

things even a world-class secret agent couldn't escape.

POISON ISLAND

DEEP WATERS

FROZEN FEAR

MIND GAMES

NIGHT RAID

TOMB OF DOOM

LUNAR STRIKE

SUDDEN DROP

BLOCKBUSTER

SHOCKWAVE

HIGH RISK

UNDERCOVER

SKY HIGH

VOLCANIC PANIC

BOOT CAMP

READING
>>> ON